This Walker book belongs to:

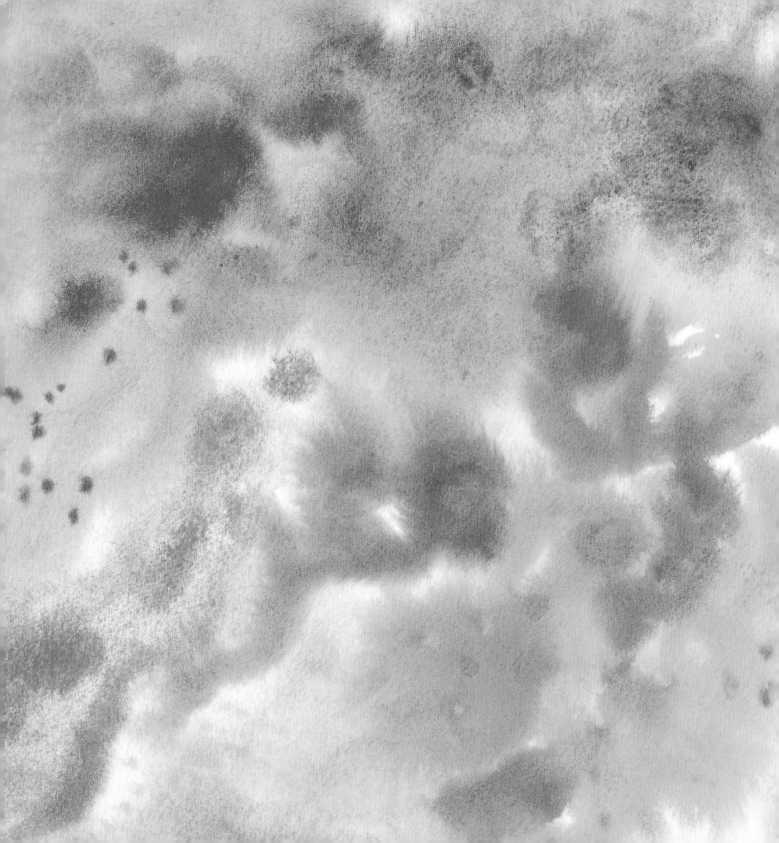

Sky colour

Peter H. Reynolds

WALKER BOOKS
AND SUBSIDIARIES
LONDON • BOSTON • SYDNEY • AUCKLAND

Marisol was an artist.
She loved to draw and paint,
and she even had her very
own art gallery.

Not all her art hung in a gallery.
Much of it she shared
with the world.

SAVE THE
OCEAN

GET WELL

She painted posters
to share ideas she
believed in.

At school, Marisol was famous for
her creative clothes, her box of art materials
and her belief that everybody was an artist.

Yes, Marisol was an artist through and through. So when her teacher told the class they were going to paint a mural for the library, Marisol couldn't wait to begin.

The classroom buzzed with the sound of brainstorming. The students talked and sketched. Together they made a great big drawing.

Then they marched to the library.
"I'll paint a fish!" "I'll paint one, too."
"I'll paint the sea!"
Marisol shouted, "I'll paint the sky!"

Marisol rummaged through the box
of paints but could not find any blue.

"How am I going to make the sky without blue paint?"

The bell rang. It was time to put their brushes down for the day. As she climbed aboard the bus, Marisol kept wondering.

All the way home, she
stared out of the window.

The sun sank closer to the horizon.

Later, at home, Marisol watched day turn into night.

That night, Marisol settled
into a deep dream.

She drifted through a sky swirling with colours.
The colours mixed, making too many to count.

In the morning, Marisol stood
waiting for the bus in the rain.
The sky was not blue.
She smiled.

At school, Marisol raced to the library.
She grabbed a dish and began adding colours.
This one, that one. She swirled the brush
to make an altogether new colour.

Marisol then began painting on the wall.
A boy asked, "What colour is THAT?"
"That?" Marisol said. "THAT is sky colour."

Dedicated to Aldo Servino,
who took the blue paint away
from me and helped me paint —
and think — in sky colour

First published 2013 by Walker Books Ltd
87 Vauxhall Walk, London SE11 5HJ

This edition published 2014

2 4 6 8 10 9 7 5 3 1

© 2012 Peter H. Reynolds

The right of Peter H. Reynolds to be identified as author/illustrator of this work has been
asserted by him in accordance with the Copyright, Designs and Patents Act 1988

This book has been hand-lettered by Peter H. Reynolds

Printed in China

British Library Cataloguing in Publication Data:
a catalogue record for this book is available from the British Library

ISBN 978-1-4063-5344-0

www.walker.co.uk